Look at the Robot

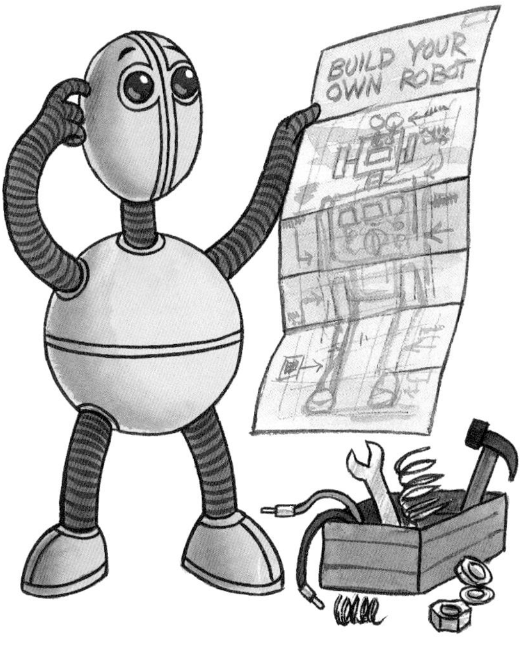

Illustrated by Dave Gunson

Rigby

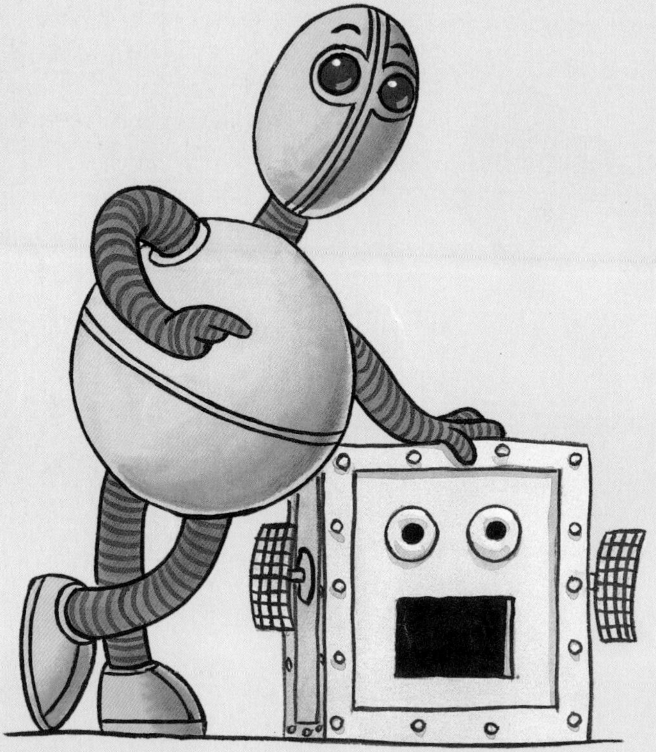

Look at the head.

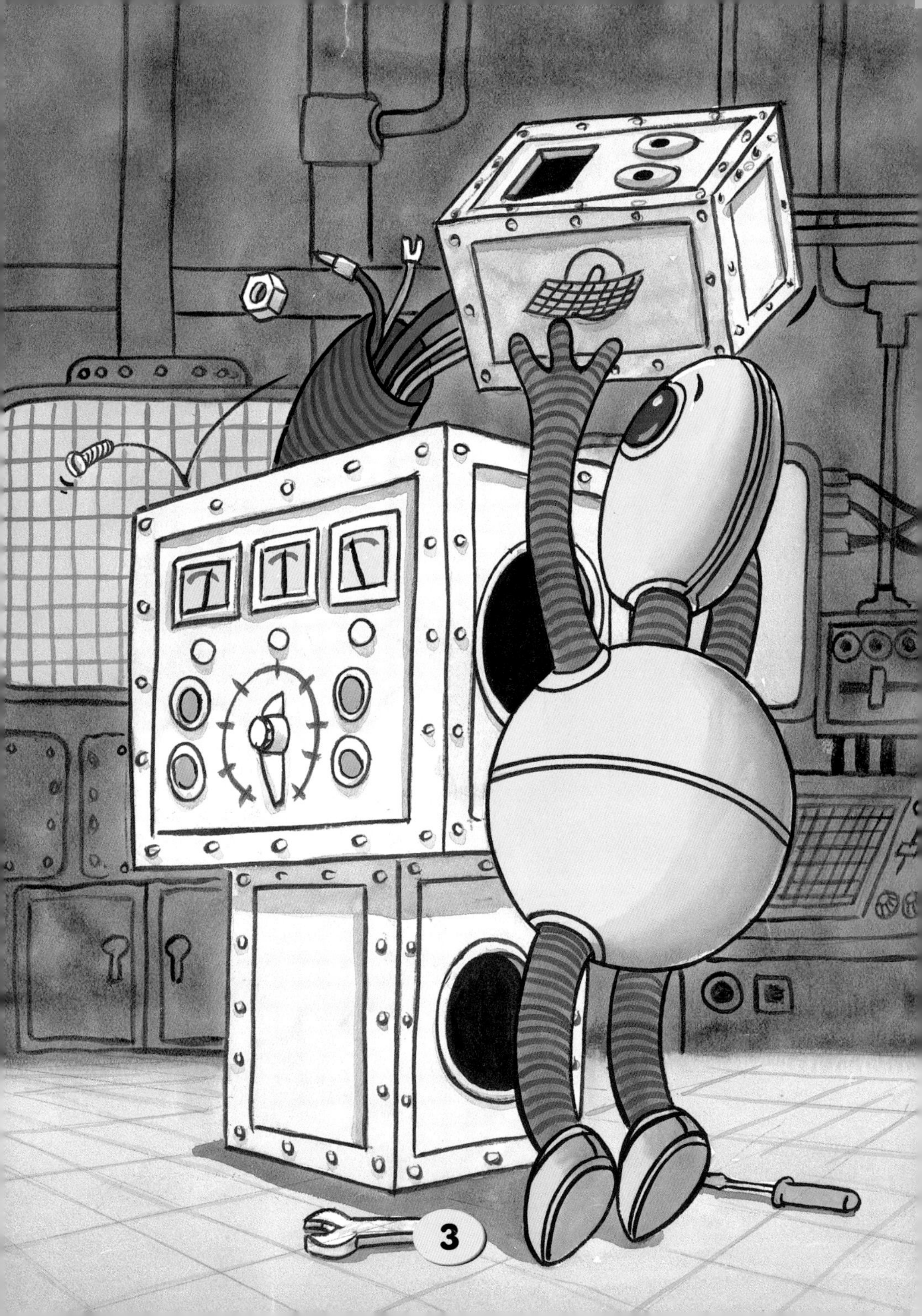

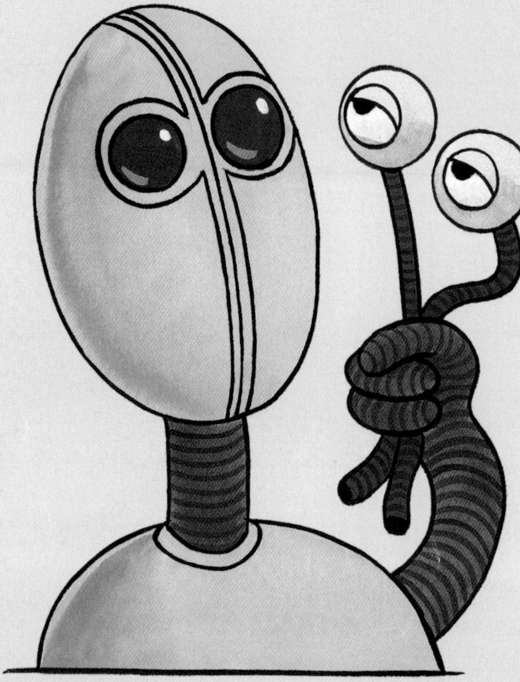

Look at the eyes.

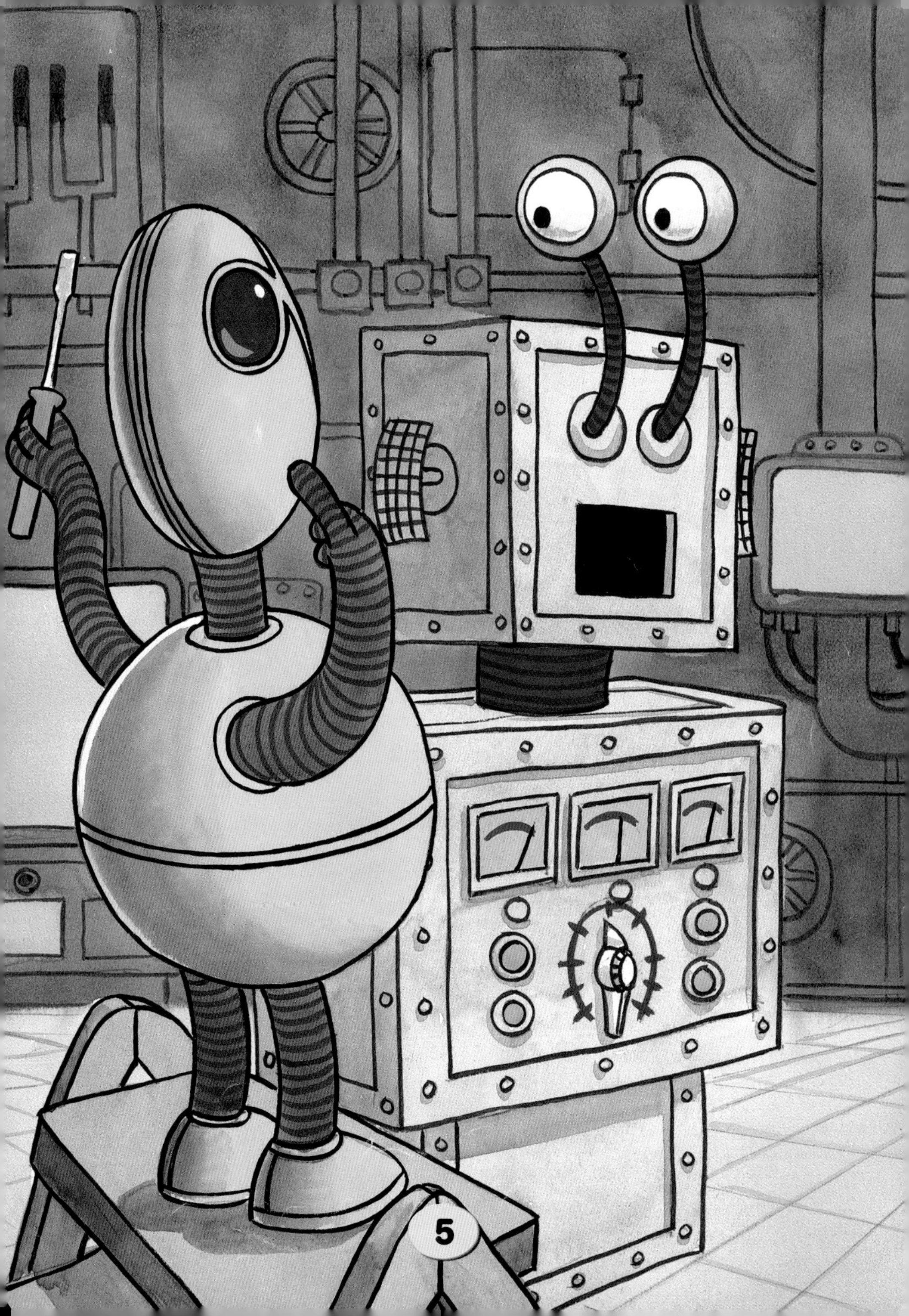

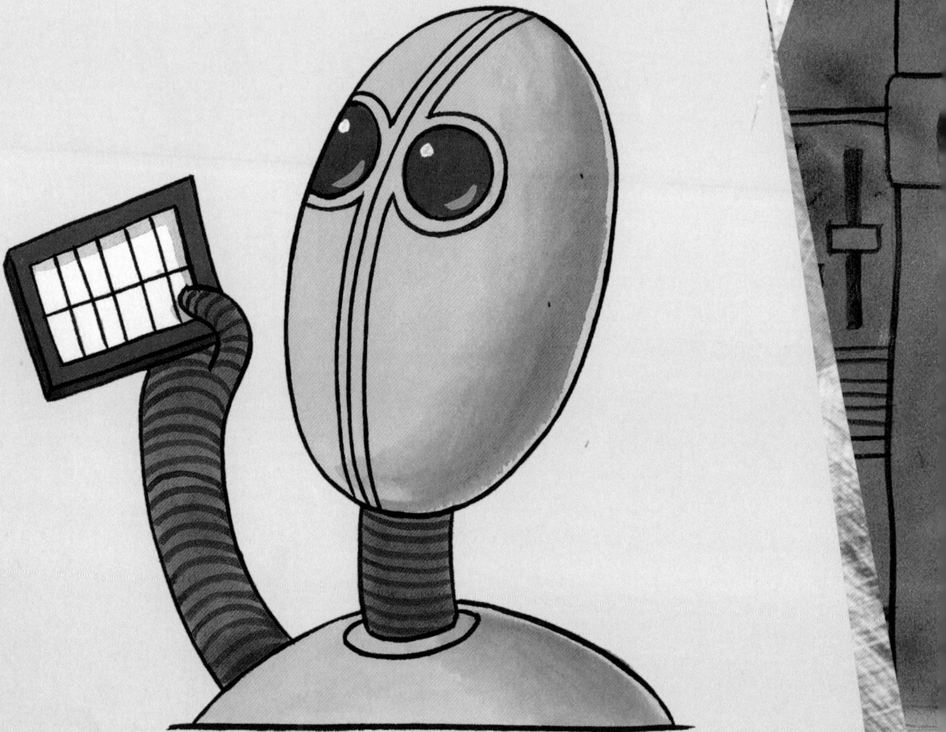

Look at the mouth.

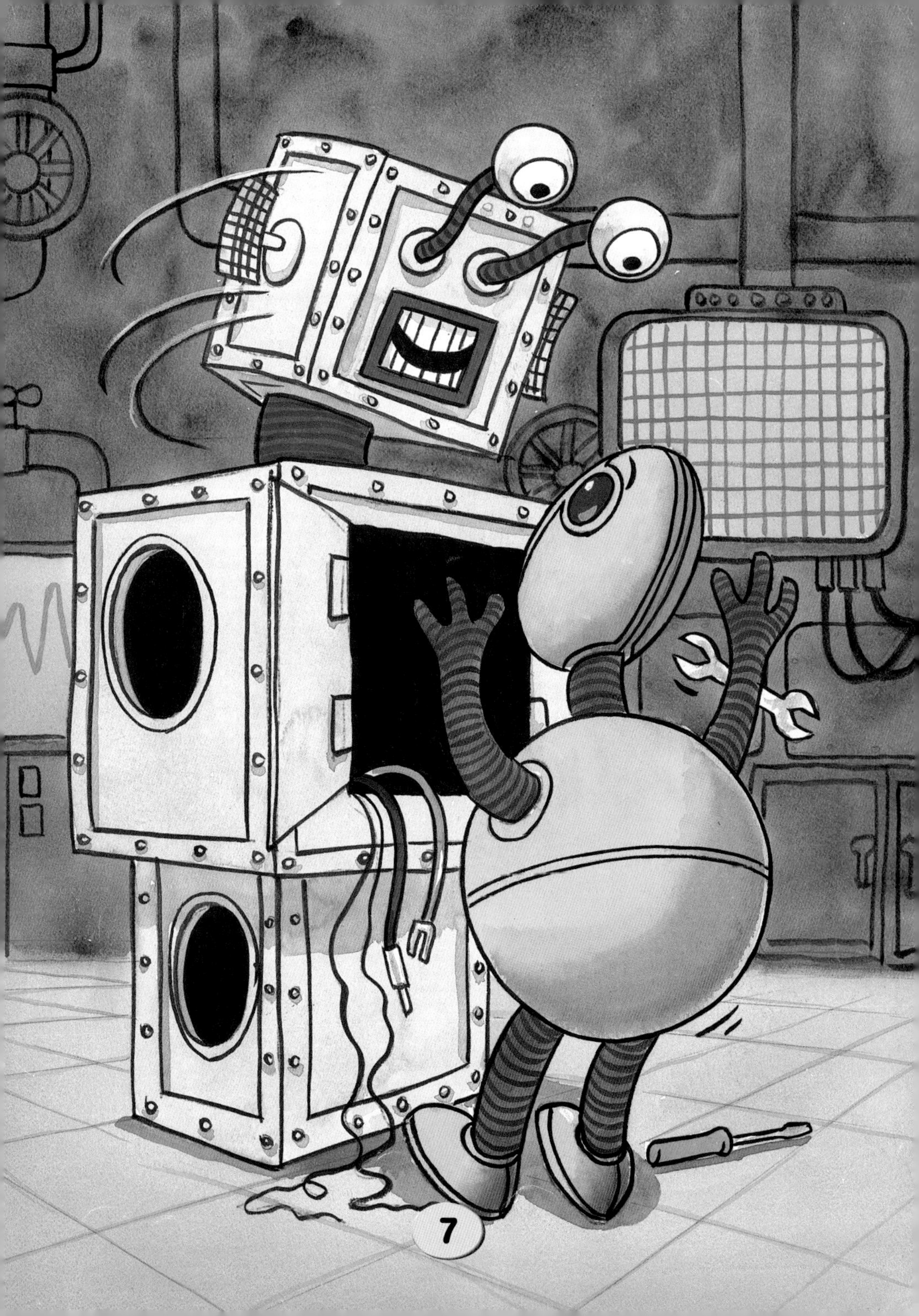

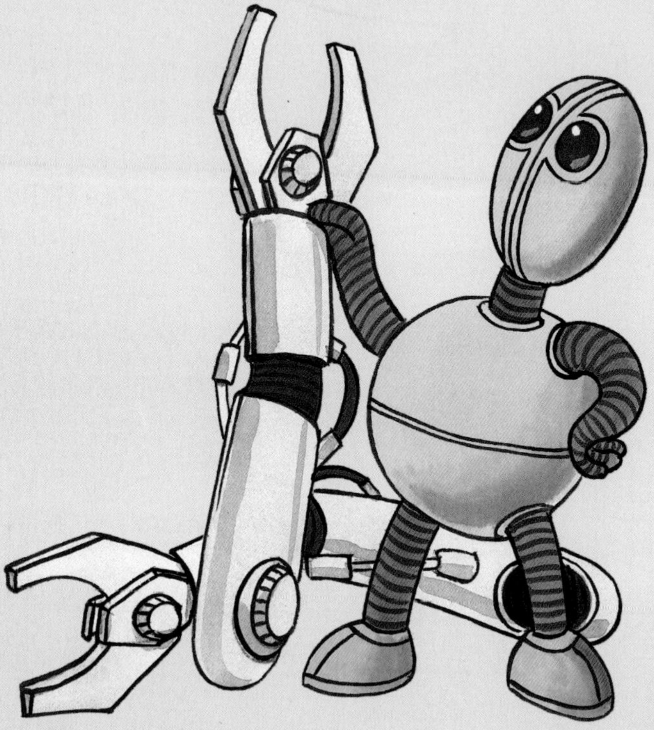

Look at the arms.

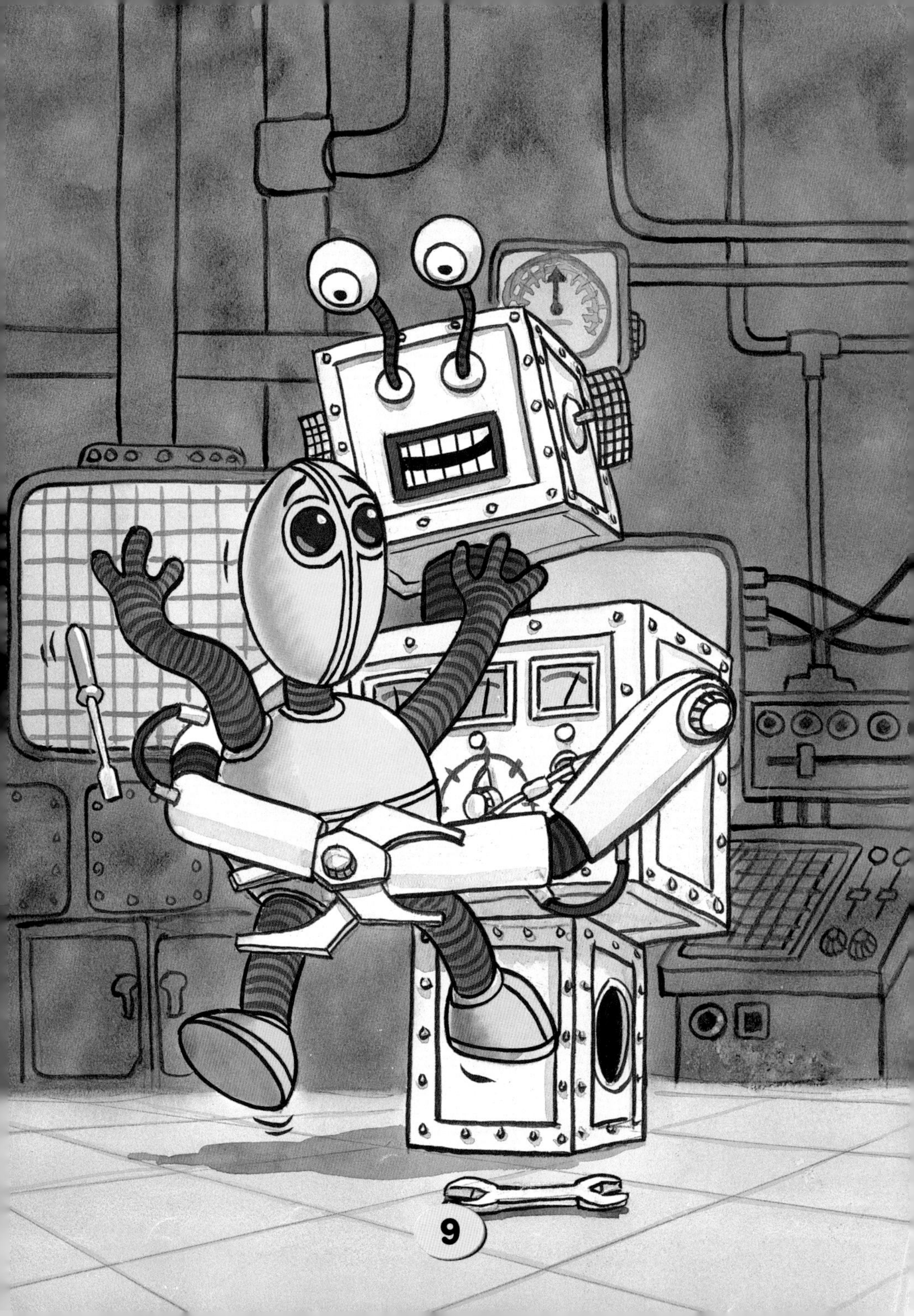

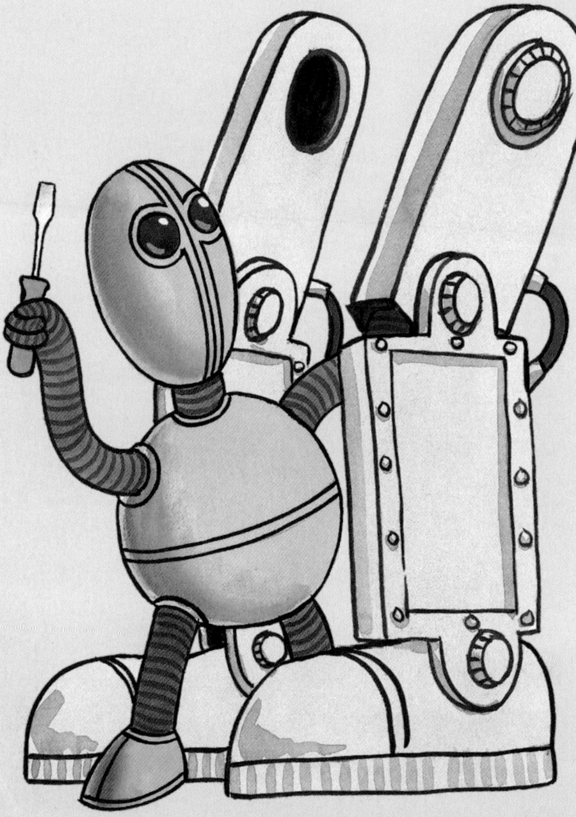

Look at the legs.

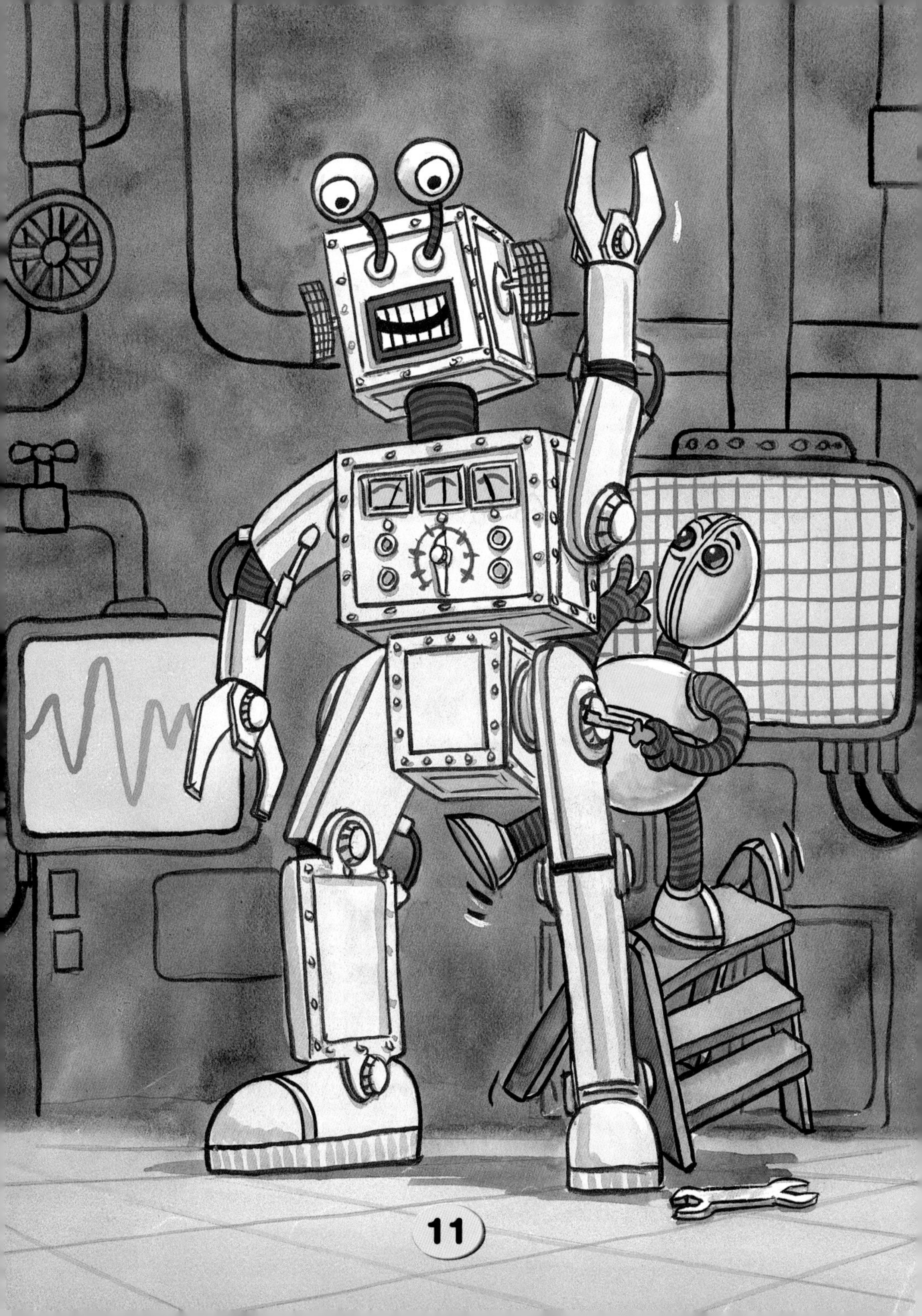

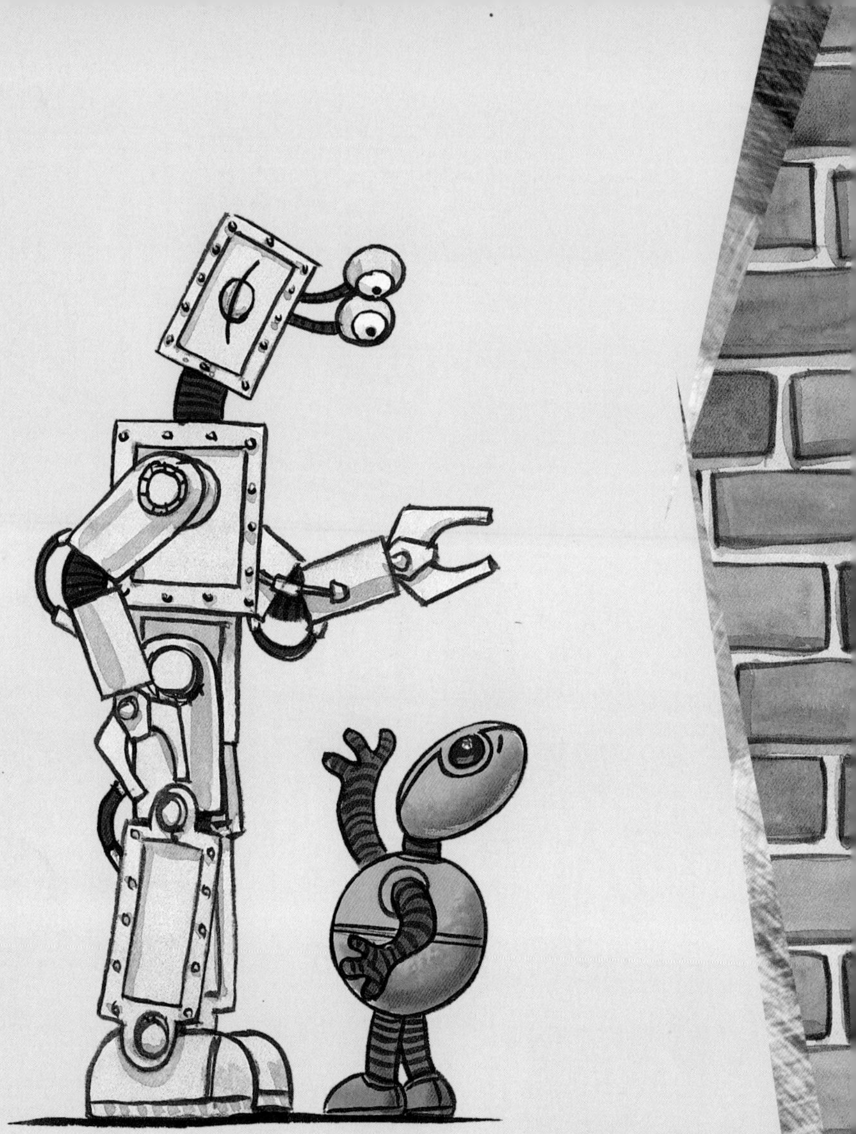

Look at the robot.

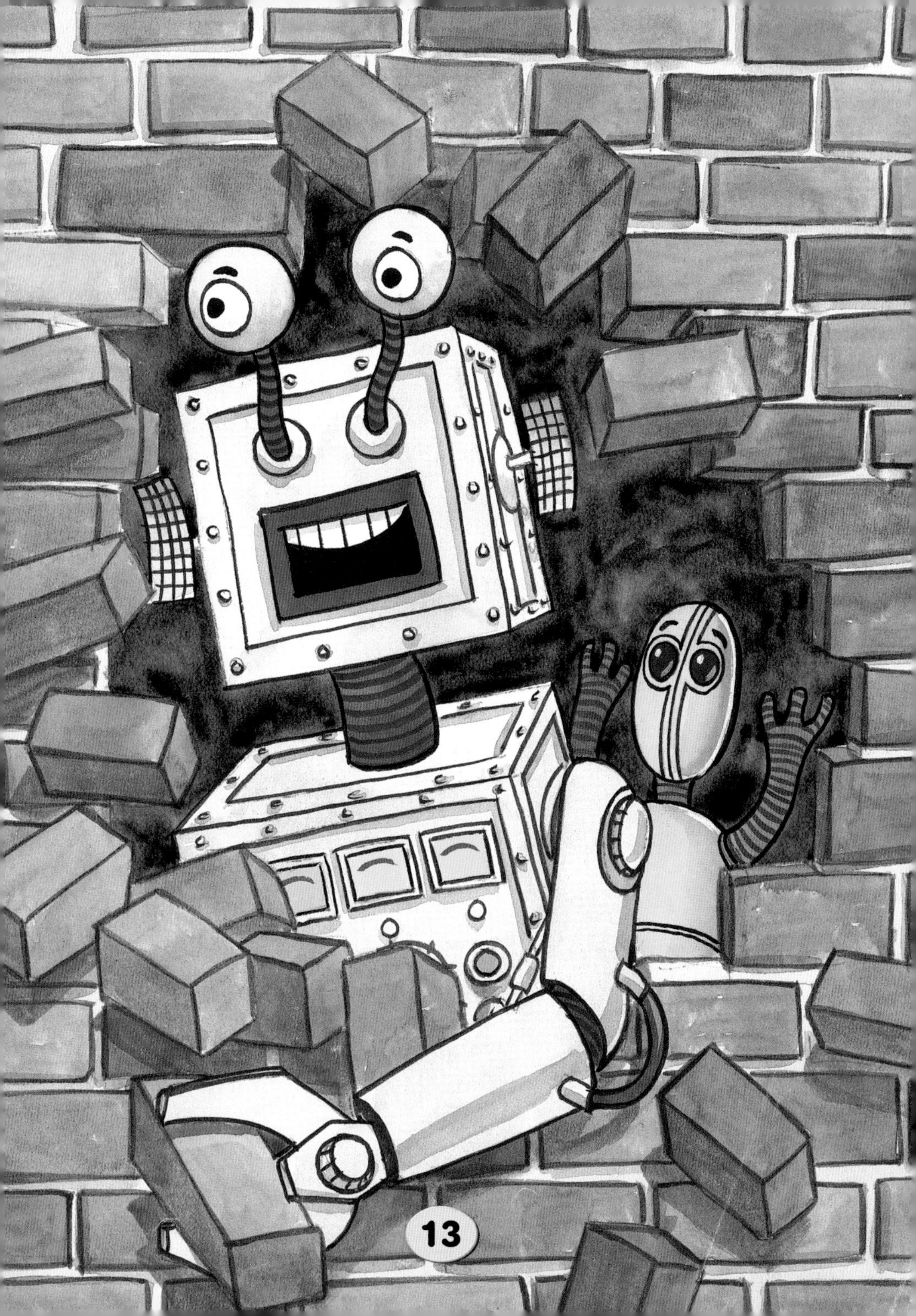

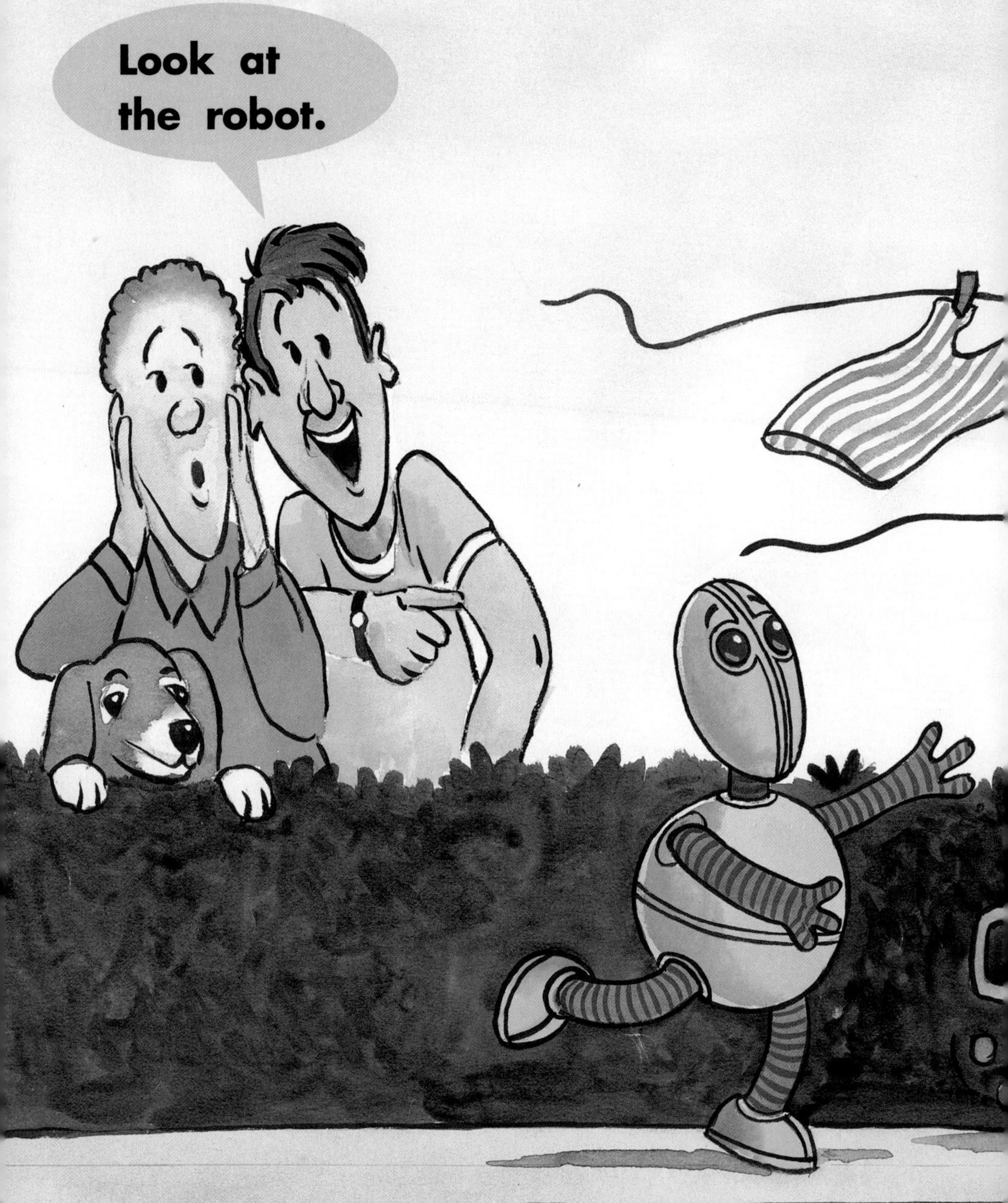
Look at the robot.

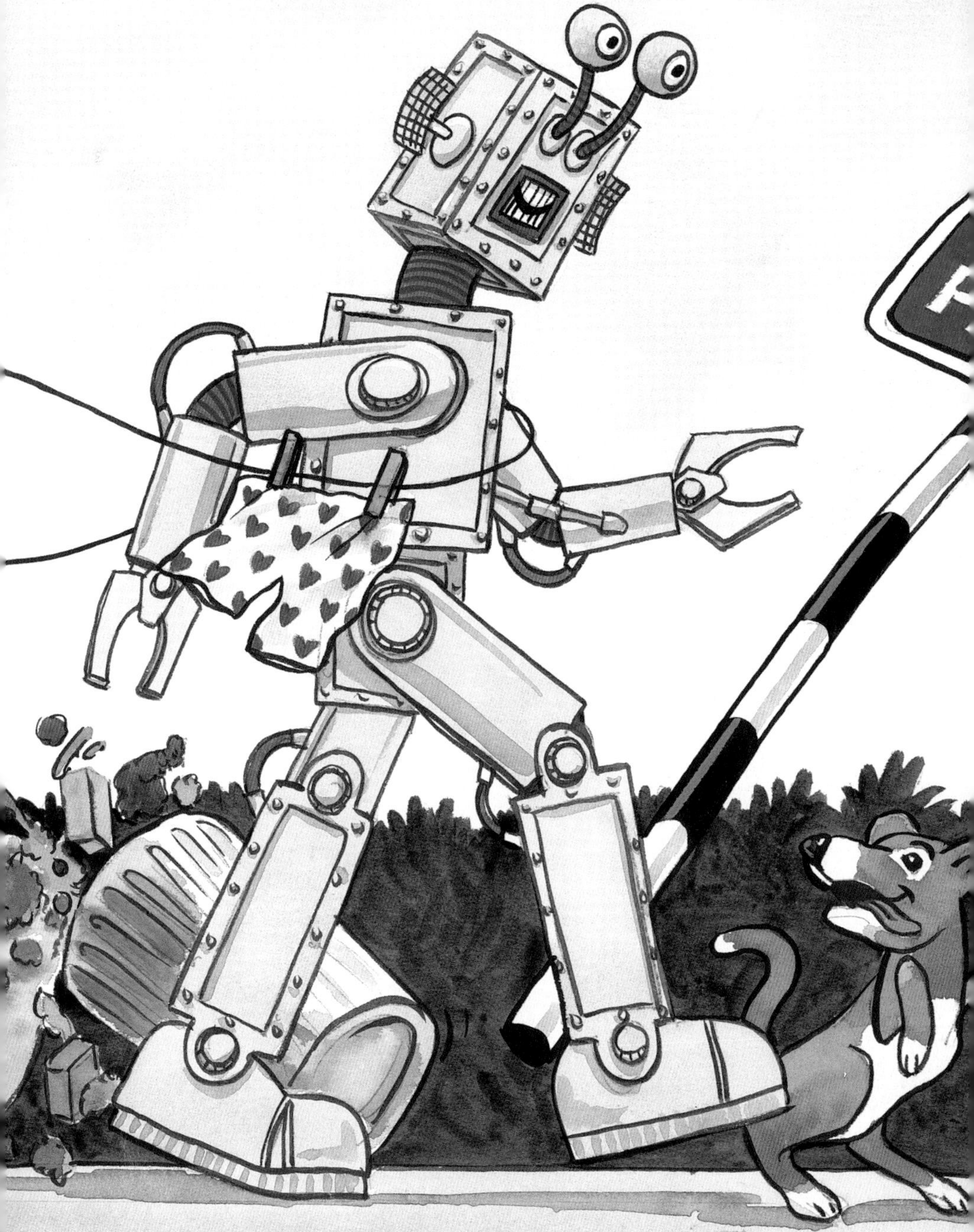

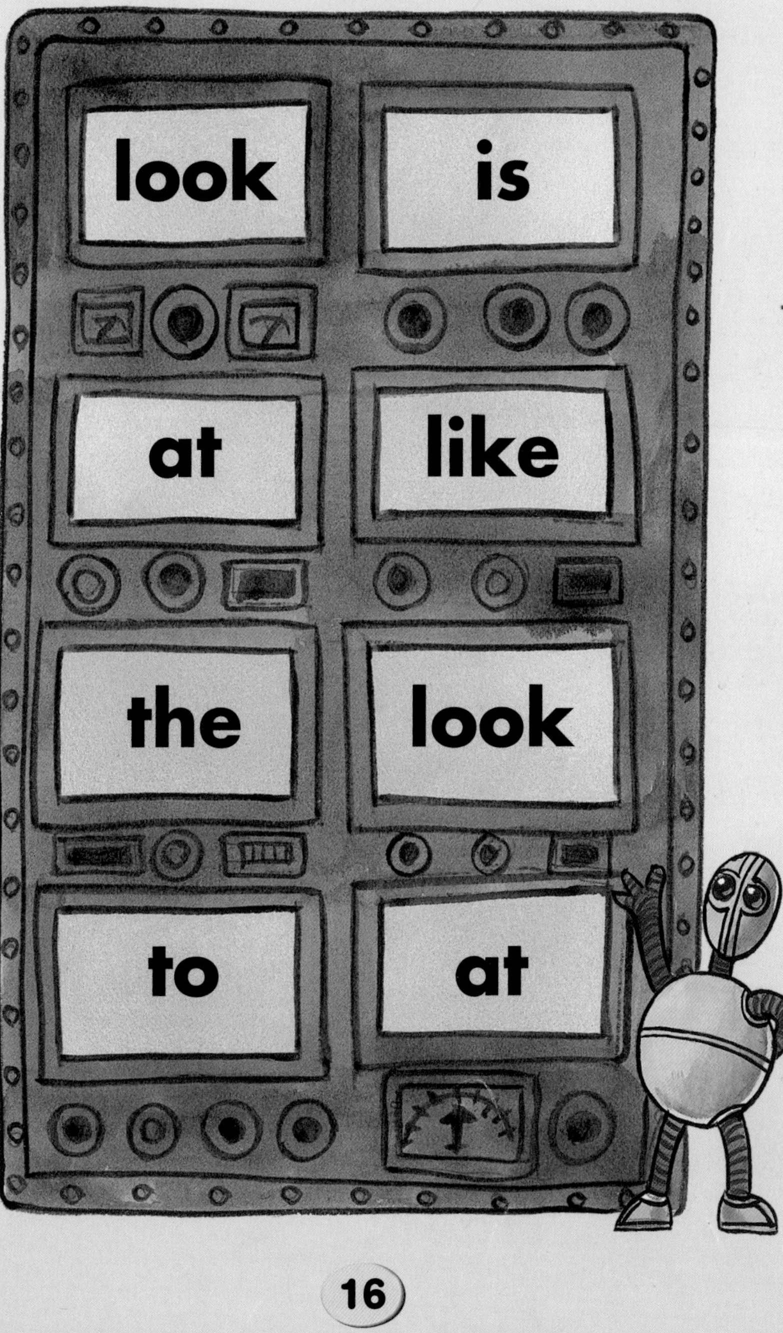
look
is
at
like
the
look
to
at